ISBN 978-1-0980-5128-0 (paperback)
ISBN 978-1-0980-0529-0 (hardcover)
ISBN 978-1-0980-0530-6 (digital)

Christian Faith Publishing, Inc.
832 Park Avenue
Meadville, PA 16335
www.christianfaithpublishing.com

Printed in the United States of America

For my children who inspire and amaze me a little more each day, and to my husband, my best friend and forever hero.

Prologue

A hero is defined as an individual who is brave, courageous, and someone to look up to. There are so many heroes that have to work on Christmas and other holidays. Military, fire fighters, doctors, paramedics, EMT's, police, correctional officers, nurses and mental health workers are just a few examples of the heroes that we know and love. Heroes need to work every day so that they can always be around to keep us safe. We thank all our special heroes who keep us safe and healthy every single day... and so does Santa.

Next week is Christmas. There is so much that I love about Christmas. I love playing with my cousins at my Nana and Pepé's, all the yummy food I get to eat, setting up the nativity scene…and presents! Everywhere I go people are smiling and excited. I should be excited too…

But instead I am sad.

My daddy has to work.

You see, my daddy is a hero. He keeps everyone safe by keeping all the naughty people away.

He is a correctional officer.

Mama walks to the bottom of the stairs. It's the third time this morning she has tried to get me out of bed.

"Time to wake up, Haddie! Hurry, hurry!"

"Ooooookkaaaay."

But I still did not hurry. Because when I'm feeling sad I'm slow like a snail.

I creep to the closet to get my clothes.

I just can't choose.

I'm sluggish as I walk down the stairs.

I don't laugh or join in as Bubba, my little brother, talks and moves like a robot.

And when my favorite cereal is given to me (rainbow unicorn puffs), my belly already feels full, and I just. Can't. Eat...

"Haddie, what's wrong? You are very slow-moving today, and you haven't touched your cereal. Are you feeling okay?"

"Oh, Mama I'm just so sad! Christmas is my favorite day of the year, but I heard you and Daddy talking. Daddy has to WORK! He won't be around to get dressed all fancy and go to church, eat yummy treats, play games, and read Christmas stories! And he won't be here to see what Santa brings us! And that makes me feel so sad, so glum, so down in the dumps, so

TERRIBLE!"

Mama looks at me, shakes her head with a knowing smile, and gives me a big tight hug.

"Oh, Haddie! You didn't know? Santa always makes special trips for heroes!"

Haddie slowly raises her head and looks perplexed.

"What do you mean?"

"You just ask!"

"You just ask? You mean…Santa will come a different day if we just ask?"

This sounds too good to be true.

"He sure will! And guess what, the Easter Bunny makes special trips too!"

"Sooo...wait...how? We can just change Christmas?" (This is weird)

"Oh, no, no, sweetie. Christmas will always be on Christmas. We can't change your birthday, just the same as we can't change Christmas. But we can change how we choose to celebrate!

We will still wake up on Christmas
morning, go to church...

eat yummy food...

and spend time with family...but sadly, Daddy
will still need to miss that this year..."

"Well, this is still sad news, Mama."

"I agree. That part is still sad. But he won't miss everything!

He won't miss the presents.

So he won't miss out on that beautiful smile of yours, and both you and Bubba's eyes lighting up as you open your gifts!

Santa knows it's sometimes tricky being a hero."

"Mama, sometimes it's tricky being
the daughter of a hero too."

"That's right, so if we fill this out completely and send it to Santa, he will come on whatever day you choose."

"Even if it's months away?"

"Even if it's months away."

"Even if it's the day before?"

"Even if it's the day before."

"Even if it's on MY birthday?"

"I'm sure he will! Here let's fill this out! We just need to tell him what day we will be home and the reason for the new date."

My mind is blown. This feels too good to be true. I feel my mouth slowly turn into a smile as I begin to think about Daddy being able to enjoy part of Christmas with us (and that we get TWO special days). I'm still sad he will not be with us on Christmas morning, but I'm happy he won't miss out on everything.

I walk over to the desk with Mama as we fill out the special request sheet and answer all the questions.

When we are all done, I ran over to Bubba who is playing with the train set that wraps around our magical Christmas tree. Now I really, really cannot wait for Christmas…

And Santa's delivery day!

Special Delivery Request

Dear Santa,

My name is _____ I am _____ years old and have been a good _____. My _____ is a hero because _____. They need to work on Christmas, so I would like to request for you to visit us on a different day. Could you please visit my family on _____ instead of December 25th? Some things that I have done lately that I am proud of are _____. I would really like it if you could bring me _____.

Thank you!

Sincerely,

About the Author

Jennifer McAdoo, LMHC is a licensed mental health therapist who works with young children and their families. She also has two young children of her own and is married to their hero. Her children's favorite holiday has always been Christmas, and they very much look forward to their visit from Santa every year. Being in a "hero family" inspired Jennifer to write this story. She hopes it helps other families as much as it has helped her own.